Doggone Lemonade Stand!

Judy Bradbury

Illustrations by Cathy Trachok

LEARNING TRIANGLE PRESS
An imprint of McGraw-Hill

New York   San Francisco   Washington, D.C.   Auckland   Bogotá   Caracas   Lisbon   London   Madrid
Mexico City   Milan   Montreal   New Delhi   San Juan   Singapore   Sydney   Tokyo   Toronto

Dedication

For Elmer and Lois Bradbury,
who have enriched my life beyond measure.

To Judith Terrill-Breuer, my deepest appreciation
for her integrity, her honesty, her heart,
and for giving wings to my dream.

McGraw-Hill

*A Division of The **McGraw·Hill** Companies*

1 2 3 4 5 6 7 8 9 KGP/KGP 9 0 3 2 1 0 9 8

ISBN 0-07-007042-3

McGraw-Hill books are available at special quantity discounts to use as premiums and sales promotions.
For more information, please write to the Director of Special Sales, McGraw-Hill, 11 West 19th Street, New York, NY 10011. Or contact your local bookstore.

Acquisitions editor: Judith Terrill-Breuer
Teacher review: Sharon Hixon
Designer: Jaclyn J. Boone

"It's the hottest day of the year, and there's no ice cream!" Christopher groaned. He opened the refrigerator door for some cool air.

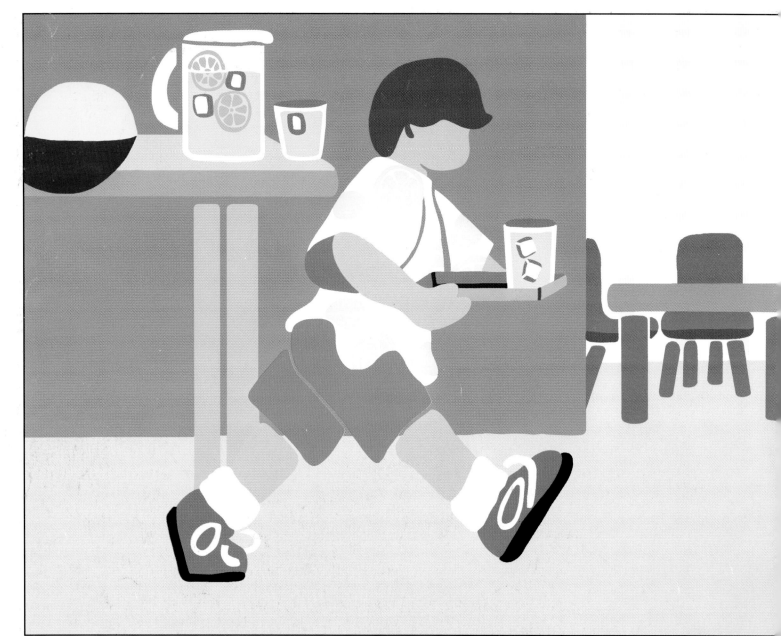

"There's no ice cream," said Mom.
"But we do have lemonade."
Christopher reached for the glistening pitcher
and filled two glasses. He took one to Mom.

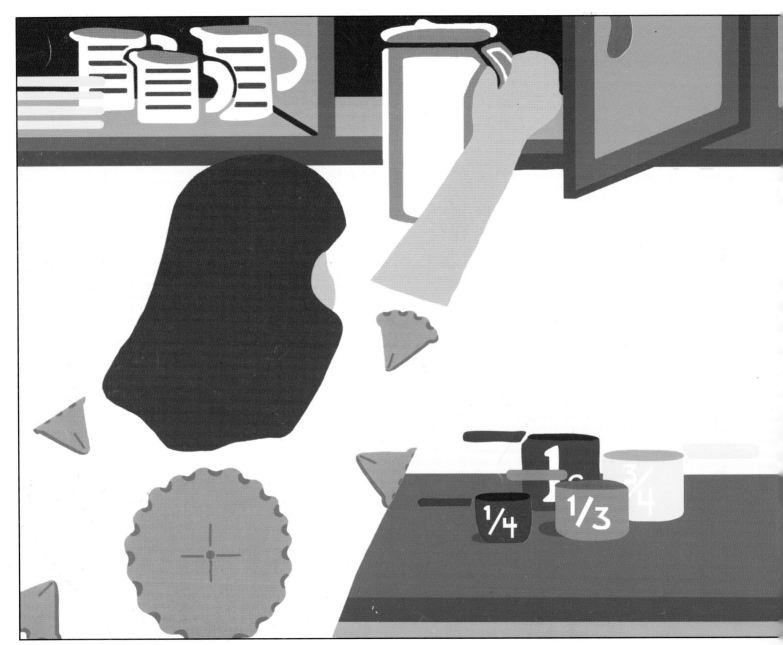

"How do you make lemonade?" he asked.

"Easy-peasy," Mom answered.

"I think I'll open a lemonade stand," Christopher said. "Then I'll have enough money so I can buy ice cream from Mrs. Cool's truck this afternoon."

"Good idea," said Mom. She reached into the cupboard for measuring cups, a plastic pitcher, and a battered, splattered recipe.

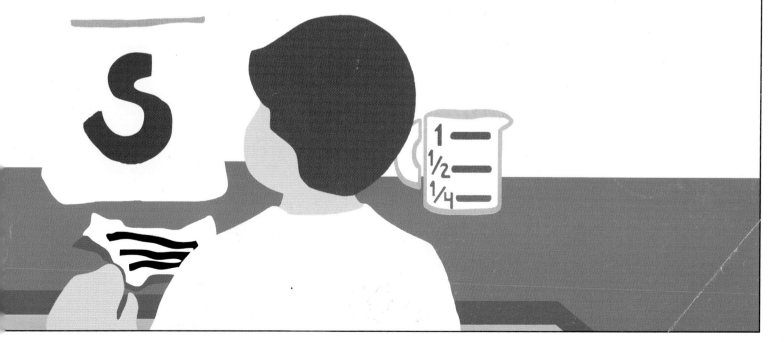

Christopher read the recipe.

3 cups of water.

He filled the 1-cup measure three times.

1 cup of lemon juice (about 4 lemons).

"I'll supply the lemons," Mom said.

1/2 cup of sugar.

He rooted through the cups,
but there was no 1/2-cup measure.

Christopher watched Mom cut a lemon in half and then cut each half again. When she was done, she had four wedges. Four quarters.

"Four quarters make a whole, so two quarters make a half." Christopher smiled and filled the 1/4 cup twice to get 1/2 cup of sugar.

Just then Christopher's little brother Jeffrey burst into the kitchen. "Me, too!" he shouted.

"Please," Mom prompted.

"You're welcome!" he answered.

Christopher eyed Jeffrey's table and chair. Just right for a lemonade stand, he thought.

Christopher's first customer
was his brother Anthony.
Next, Rosie dropped her
mail sack to look for change.
"Delightful," declared the meter reader.
"Per-fecto," proclaimed Mom's friend Louise.
Clink-clink went the coins in the cup.

Making money's a cinch, Christopher thought. He looked up the block for Mrs. Cool's ice cream truck. Instead, he saw Carmella Sanchez.

She flipped her skateboard under her arm and sauntered over. "You're only half full," she said, pointing to the pitcher. "I'll watch the stand while you make more. For a nickel."

Inside, Christopher found a bowl
of lemon wedges in the refrigerator.
He counted out four quarters, 16 times.
Lemons lined the counter.

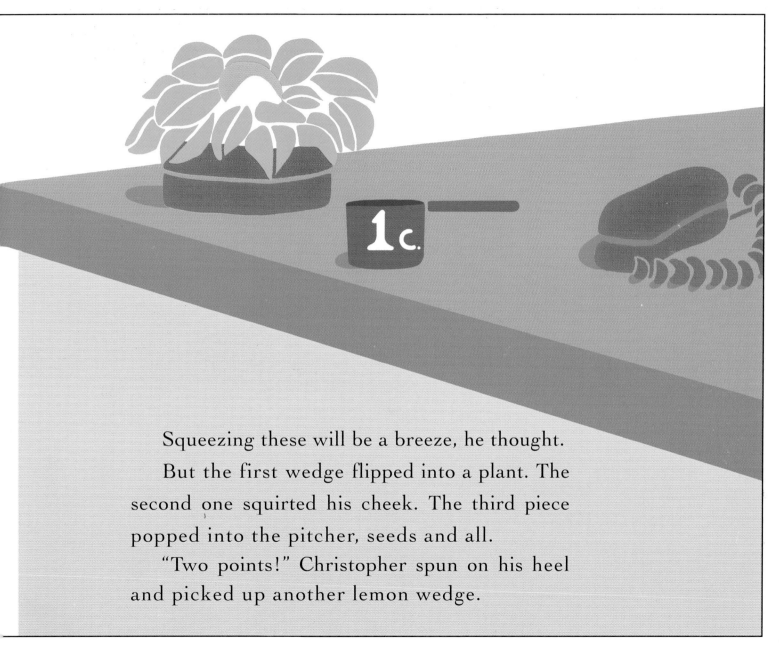

Squeezing these will be a breeze, he thought.

But the first wedge flipped into a plant. The second one squirted his cheek. The third piece popped into the pitcher, seeds and all.

"Two points!" Christopher spun on his heel and picked up another lemon wedge.

Finally, all the lemon quarters were squished, squashed, or squirted. Christopher was just about to add sugar when the phone rang. He jumped and sugar showered the kitchen. He reached for the sponge. But when he swiped at the sugar, it turned gooey and gluey.

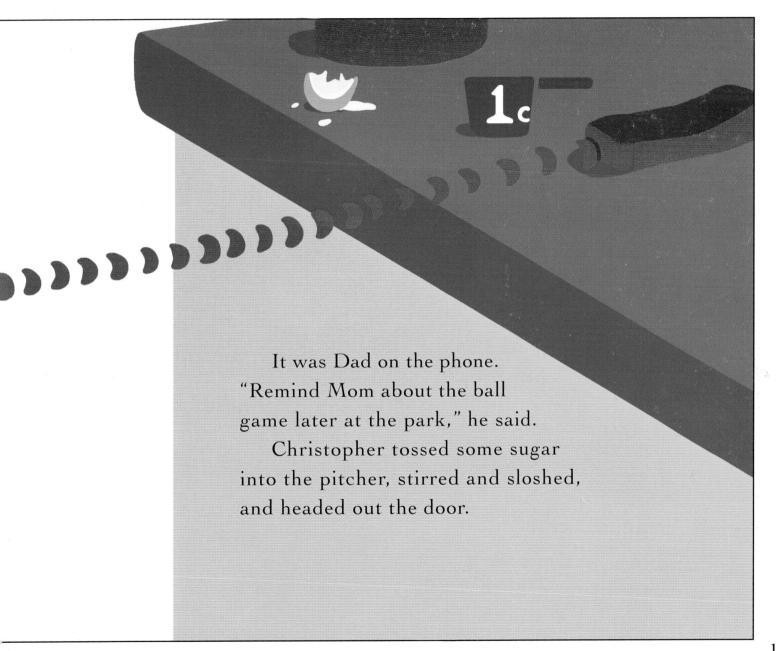

It was Dad on the phone.
"Remind Mom about the ball
game later at the park," he said.
Christopher tossed some sugar
into the pitcher, stirred and sloshed,
and headed out the door.

There was Doofus, the neighborhood dog.

"Get away from my lemonade stand!" Christopher yelped.
He grabbed the garden hose.

"My lemonade won't be safe until that dog is gone," said Christopher.

Anthony snapped his fingers. "I have the perfect name for your business—The Doggone Lemonade Stand!"

That's when Christopher noticed Carmella's note.

Christopher, you took too long.
Thanks for the nickel. P.S. Your
lemonade needs more sugar.

Christopher sighed and sat down on Jeffrey's too-small chair to wait for customers. The ice melted, the pitcher beaded with sweat, and so did Christopher.

No one came.

"Whoever said making money's a cinch?" he muttered. "Maybe my sign is the problem."

"That looks good," said a voice behind him.

Christopher turned. "Want to buy some lemonade?"

"We just moved in and I haven't unpacked my bank yet. But I'll trade you this cookie for a glass of lemonade."

It wasn't money, but it had been a long time since breakfast. "Deal!" said Christopher.

The boy drained his glass. "I'm Byron," he said, "and this is great!"

Christopher broke the cookie in half. "My name's Christopher. Let's share."

He was just about to take a bite when the screen door opened.

"Mine!" shrieked Jeffrey, pointing to his table and chair.

Christopher had to act fast. "Want some?" he asked, breaking his half of the cookie in half. 1/4 cookie was better than nothing, he figured.

"Don't forget me!" said Anthony.
Byron grinned. "I'll share this time."

They were working on a new sign when Rachel came by.

"Lemonade for sale!" said Christopher.

"Carmella says it needs more sugar," said Rachel.

"This is Byron," said Christopher, "and he thinks it's great."

Rachel pulled a pack of markers out of her pocket. "Can I have a glass if I help with the sign? We can use my markers."
"Deal!" said Christopher.

They were just finishing the sign when Joey rode by.

"That lemonade looks good," he said, "but Carmella says it needs more sugar."

"This is Byron," said Rachel, "and he thinks it's great."

"I'll trade half of my balloons for a glass," said Joey.

"Deal," said Christopher.

Just then, Mrs. Cool went by.

"Can't stop now!" she called out the window. "I'm headed for the park!"

"That's it!" shouted Christopher. "Pack up the wagon!"

"One lemonade for me, please," said Joey's father.

"Tastes great!" said Dad.

"Just needs a little more sugar," said Mrs. Sanchez.

Clink-clink went the coins in the cup.

When the game was over, Christopher was
all out of lemonade. But he had plenty of money.

So much money that he bought an
ice cream cone for each of his friends . . .

. . . even Doofus.

Discoveries

You can read this story, and you can count it, too!

Page 1: Find the one-gallon jug. A gallon is four quarts (think **quarters**). Find the 1/2 gallon container. How many quarts are there in 1/2 gallon?

Pages 4-5: Look at the measuring cups. Which is the biggest? Smallest?

Page 6: Where is the 1/2 cup measure?

Page 7: Four quarters make a whole, so two quarters make a half. *Tricky math!* How many quarters are there in **two** lemons?

Pages 10–11: How much money has Christopher made so far?

Page 14: Christopher counted out four quarters four times. How many lemon wedges does he have? *Tricky math!* How many whole lemons does it take to make 16 quarters?

Page 21: How much money does Christopher have left?

Page 33: Joey has 8 unfilled ballons. He offers Christopher **half** of them. How many does he have left?

Page 36: There are 16 spokes on Joey's bike. Half of them are on the front wheel and half of them are on the back wheel. What is **half** of 16?

Page 42–44: If Mrs. Cool's ice cream cones cost 50 cents, or **half** a dollar, each, how much money does Christopher need to buy a cone for each of his friends? (Don't forget Doofus!) If ice cream cones cost 25 cents, or a **quarter,** each, how much money does Christopher need?

Don't miss the other *Christopher Counts* books . . .

One Carton of Oops!
Double Bubble Trouble!
A High-Fiving Gift for Mom!